Hedgerow
Tales

For Jonathan and Peter

Copyright © 1984 Pat Wynnejones

Published by
Lion Publishing plc
Icknield Way, Tring, Herts, England
ISBN 0 85648 596 9
Lion Publishing Corporation
1705 Hubbard Avenue, Batavia, Illinois 60510, USA
ISBN 0 85648 596 9
Albatross Books Pty Ltd
PO Box 320, Sutherland, NSW 2232, Australia
ISBN 0 86760 490 5

First edition 1984
Reprinted 1985, 1987

Printed and bound in Singapore

THE STORY OF
Benjamin Bee

Retold by Pat Wynnejones
from Mrs Gatty's 'Parables of Nature'

Illustrated by Sandra Fernandez

A LION BOOK

Benjamin was a happy working bee. He enjoyed collecting honey from the flowers and taking it back to the hive. He liked being busy.

One lovely summer morning the sun was shining so brightly and the air felt so warm that he left the hive and flew a long, long distance. He came to a garden where the flowers were very beautiful and sweet with nectar. He worked hard among the hollyhocks and canterbury bells and soon had his honey sacs full. As he was carefully backing out of a foxglove bell, he overheard two grass-hoppers talking. He soon realized that they were making remarks about him.

'Look at that worker bee slaving away,' said one of them.

'He must be stupid to work so hard,' said the other. 'The Queen Bee just lies at home doing nothing. Why doesn't he try staying at home?'

Benjie was surprised. He had never thought of that before. He had never envied the Queen. He was happy, so why shouldn't he do the work he enjoyed?

'Nobody,' twittered the first grasshopper, jumping up and down; 'Nobody,' he sang, leaping high in the air; 'Nobody sensible would work, when they could spend their day singing and playing as we do.'

'That's funny,' thought Benjie anxiously. 'Perhaps I am peculiar. I hope there's nothing wrong with me. I really do enjoy my work.'

'He must be stupid! Tee-hee! He must be unhappy! Tra-la-la!'

The grasshoppers squeaked and jigged an aggravating dance, and as Benjie emerged from the foxglove they shouted rude things at him.

'Stupid am I?' thought poor Benjie. 'Just because I love flying from flower to flower in the sun, instead of doing nothing all day? And am I unhappy?'

As Benjie flew home the bright day seemed darker. He began to wonder. Did the Queen really have a better time than he did? Was she much more important? And what about the drones? Were they better off than he was? Were the honey-gatherers like him simply stupid, doing the hard work because they were neither the Queen nor the dignified drones?

When he arrived back at the hive he asked an Aged Relation some of these questions.

His Aged Relation buzzed and stuttered. 'Well, tell me, young bee, are you feeling unhappy?'

'Well, yes, I am rather,' admitted poor Benjie.

'Bzz,' continued the Aged Relation, 'were you feeling unhappy when you set out this morning?'

'No, indeed not. I was full of the joy of the sunshine and breezes and wonderful scent of the flowers.'

'Bzz. I see. And are you usually unhappy when you go collecting?'

'No. I just love collecting honey. It's fun!'

'Umm — zzz,' stuttered the Aged Relation. 'Then my judgement in the matter is this. You never were unhappy until someone told you that you were. And my advice is — ignore it. Yes, my bee, ignore it and be happy. Typical grasshopper talk, typical grasshopper talk. Be yourself. Be...be...zzz.' And the Aged Relation drowsed into a mumbling snore and dozed off.

Benjie could still not shake off the horrid feeling that the grasshoppers had given him. Maybe he was happy — but they had also called him stupid. Was he stupid?

So he flew about until he found some of his friends. They gathered together among the brilliant orange and gold nasturtium flowers and he told them the whole story. When he had finished there was a confused buzzing as each bee tried to express an opinion. They made so much noise that they awoke the Aged Relation. He flew up just in time to hear one of them speaking.

'All bees should be Queens,' said the bee and a great cheer went up.

'Bzz,' murmured the Aged Relation. 'What would be the fun of being a Queen if there were no working bees waiting on you?'

'Then we should all be drones,' suggested another bee.

'Bzz — and who would make the honey and wax and build the honeycombs and nurse the children?'

'Maybe all bees should be worker bees?' asked a small puzzled bee in a small puzzled voice.

'And would that help you?' asked the Aged Relation. 'Bzz — it seems to me that you are worker bees already.' And away he buzzed, tired of the chattering.

The argument had stirred up a lot of bad feeling and discontent. None of them wanted to go collecting, although the sun was still high.

Then Benjie had a bright idea. 'Let's go off and start a hive of our own,' he said, 'where each one does anything he pleases. We'll all be alike and equal.' Then he thought for a moment and added, 'But I'll be the leader.'

So it was agreed and off they flew, Benjie in the lead. But while he was trying to decide where to settle for their hive the others flew on past him.

'Hi, come back,' he shouted, 'I'm your leader!'

'You're not a real leader,' one of the big ones jeered over his shoulder. 'You're not a Queen. You don't know where to choose for a hive, nor where to swarm properly!'

'Where shall we swarm?' asked the small puzzled bee nervously.

'A garden, of course,' buzzed one.

'A field,' said another.

'There is nothing like a good hollow tree,' remarked a third.

'The roof of an outhouse is best,' thought a fourth.

'The branch of a tree,' cried a fifth.

And they all shouted, 'My idea's best. I won't give way to anybody!'

'I'm very angry with you,' buzzed Benjie. 'Half the day has gone already and here we are, just as unsettled as when we started out. I'm your leader! Do as I say!'

'You're not our leader. We're all alike — we're all leaders!' they shouted, and they buzzed so fiercely that Benjie decided to leave them.

Benjie flew off sadly. And he flew a long way till he came to the beautiful garden. And as he flew among the foxgloves and hollyhocks and canterbury bells he gradually felt himself becoming happier and happier. He began to fill up his honey sacs and enjoy the scent of the flowers.

'This is how I am happiest,' he thought. 'It's funny, but I really do enjoy my work.'

As the sun began to go down he turned back to the hive, pleased with his heavy load.

To his surprise, on the way home he began to meet his friends returning in twos and threes. They had quarrelled themselves tired, found nowhere to go and now seemed glad to be going back to their own familiar hive.

But as they arrived they came back to a dreadful scene. A terrible commotion was going on inside the hive.

As Benjie watched he saw a strange and fearful sight. A procession was emerging from the hive, drawing the body of the Queen.

'The Queen is dead!' they cried.

'How did it happen?' Benjie asked the Aged Relation, who had flown to his side.

'Bzz — some of the cell-keepers went off with you and your friends and while they were away a young Queen bee burst through her cell, which they should have been guarding. Of course the two Queens fought until one fell dead. The old Queen was weaker and was killed. Now there will have to be a new hive. You see — zzz — even Queens are not equal.'

'What a terrible thing,' gasped Benjie. 'It wouldn't have happened if we had not flown away today.'

'Bzz. True. You see how important it is that each bee should do the task he is fitted for, young bee. If not, the whole hive fails. Bees may have different work to do but each one is important.'

'I do see! I do, Aged Relation! And I may not be a leader, but I do know how to collect honey! I'm off!' And Benjie zoomed off into the bright summer air.

The four stories in 'Hedgerow Tales' have been retold from Mrs Gatty's 'Parables of Nature', first published in 1855. Mrs Gatty was a children's writer, and also a keen naturalist, who used stories from the world of nature to illustrate and communicate truth about God and his purposes. Each of the stories has a particular theme, based on a verse from the New Testament of the Bible.

In these modern versions, the stories have lost none of their original freshness and charm, and their message is as relevant today as when they were first written.

'The Story of Benjamin Bee' takes as its theme contentment and a willingness to use the particular gifts God has given us, so that the whole 'body' (in this case, the hive) works together. This picture of the body is used by Paul in his letter to the Corinthians: 'If the whole body were just an eye, how could it hear? And if it were only an ear, how could it smell?... God put every different part in the body just as he wanted it to be.' (1 Corinthians 12:17, 18)